To Virginia Ferry and Ken Cluen, for giving me
the story. And to Jean Hudson and Jill Pekar,
for bringing me to the words. —S.R.

For my nephew Léon. —C.G.

Text copyright © 2021 by Sybil Rosen
Jacket and illustration copyright © 2021 by Camille Garoche

All rights reserved. Published in the United States by Schwartz & Wade Books,
an imprint of Random House Children's Books, a division of Penguin Random House LLC, New York.
Schwartz & Wade Books and the colophon are trademarks of Penguin Random House LLC.

Visit us on the Web! rhcbooks.com
Educators and librarians, for a variety of teaching tools, visit us at RHTeachersLibrarians.com

Library of Congress Cataloging-in-Publication Data is available upon request.
ISBN 978-0-593-12320-1 (hc) — ISBN 978-0-593-12321-8 (lib. bdg.)
ISBN 978-0-593-12322-5 (ebook)

The text of this book is set in 16-point Belen.
The illustrations were rendered in pencil and colored digitally
Book design by Rachael Cole

MANUFACTURED IN CHINA
10 9 8 7 6 5 4 3 2 1
First Edition

CARPENTER'S HELPER

BY SYBIL ROSEN

ILLUSTRATED BY CAMILLE GAROCHE

schwartz & wade books · new york

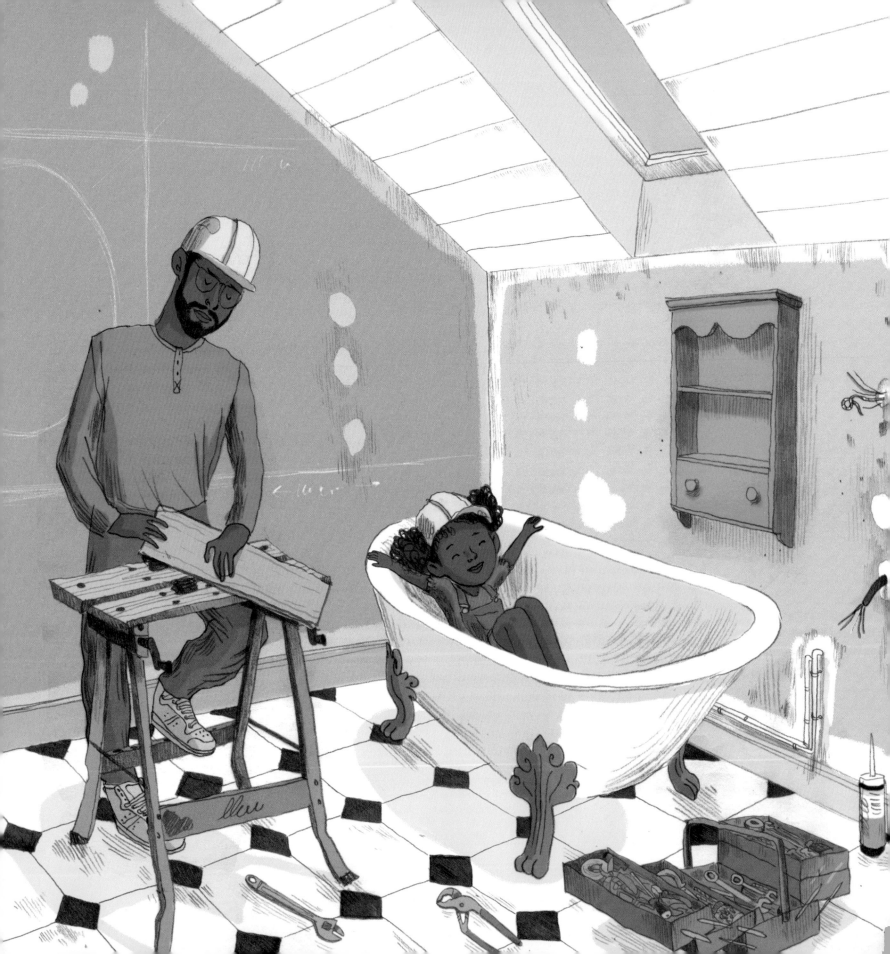

The new bathroom is halfway finished! Renata is especially excited about the deep, old-fashioned bathtub. She can already picture the castles of bubbles she will build in it.

The next job is the new window. Carefully Renata hands Papi a hammer. She holds a board while he nails it into place. This board will brace the wall when he cuts the hole for the window frame.

Renata loves the smell of sawdust. She loves looking inside the walls, where the pipes and wires live. And she loves sweeping up at the end of each day.

She finds odd treasures Papi leaves behind: A square
of painted tile. A wedge of wood. An elbow joint.
"For my carpenter's helper," he says, grinning.

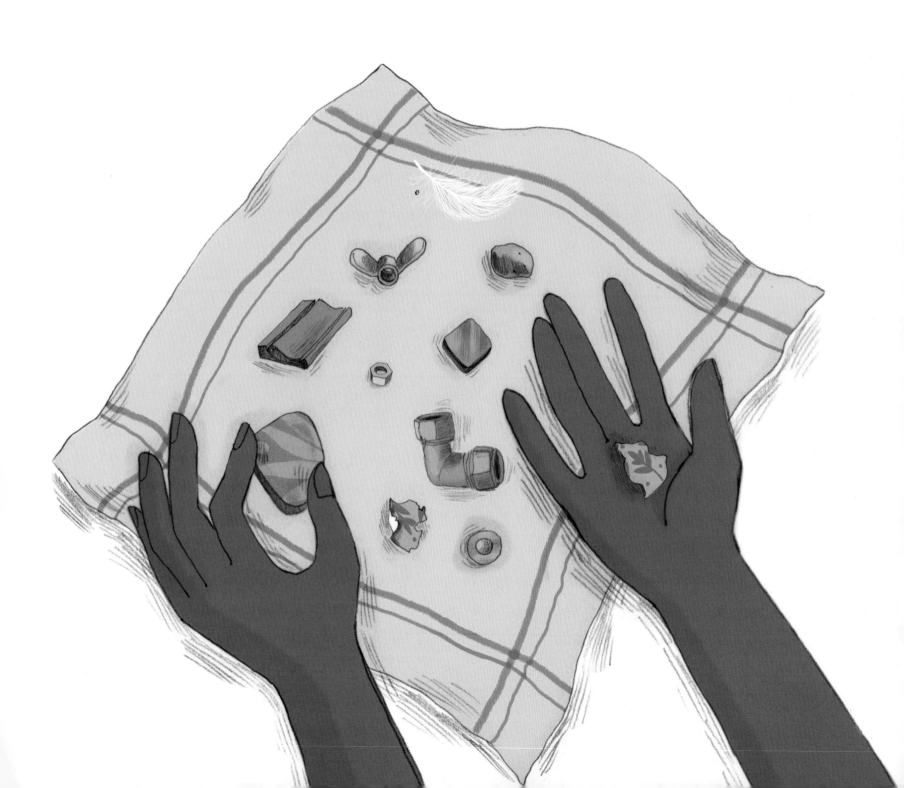

It is spring. The days are warm. One evening Papi leaves the empty window space open. The night air smells of new grass and pine straw.

The next morning Renata finds dried leaves and pine needles in the bathtub. On the wall above the tub are two small shelves. The bottom shelf is heaped with leaves and needles. How did they get there?

Whoosh! Something zips by Renata's head, inches away. She crouches down. It's a little bird—a wren!—peppy and plump, with an upturned tail. He delivers a twig to the shelf and then stops to sing about it. His song is cheerful and very loud. Renata imagines him singing, *I love my job!*

Renata watches the wren weave the leaves and needles into a nest. First he lays down a floor, a cozy cradle for eggs.

Three thick sides go up next.

On the fourth side, the wren fashions a hole as a door.

Soon mama wren wings
in to inspect the nest.

She decorates it with a scrap of moss,
a feather, a squiggle of ribbon.

Then she tucks herself down right
behind the doorway and waits.

The wrens whiz out the window just as Papi walks into the room. He eyes the nest. "Whoa. Looks like we got a visitor."

Renata giggles. "I think he's moving in."

Papi shakes his head. "We won't be able to work now. Maybe not for weeks. Can you wait that long for a bubble bath?"

"I can wait." Renata smiles up at her father. "He's a carpenter, Papi. Just like you."

Mama wren returns to the nest to lay her eggs. And day after day papa wren stays busy. He brings mama lunch. A juicy grub. Two yummy cicadas. Sometimes he sits on the windowsill and sings and sings and sings.

A week goes by. One afternoon mama and papa fly out together. Renata can hear their duet in the yard. She sneaks over to the nest. Inside are four rosy eggs with red-brown blotches.

A second week passes. Once, when mama is off the nest, Renata steals another peek. The eggs have started to split open, like coats that are suddenly too small.

The baby wrens are hatching! Each newborn chick is curled up, pink and featherless. They give Renata a shivery feeling.

The next day, Renata and Papi spy the wrens
carrying bits of eggshell out of the nest. Papi
winks. "Won't be long now."

"Till what?" Renata wonders.

"Till we can finish our bathroom."

"But then they'll be leaving." Renata frowns.

"I want them to live in our
bathroom forever."

Every day mama and papa wren fly out and back, returning each time with mouthfuls of bugs. The nestlings sing an eating song, like happy bells ringing. Renata can see their tiny heads bobbing in the nest. Soon they have their first feathers, fuzzy and gray.

Two weeks fly by. Early one morning Renata slips into the bathroom. Mama and papa wren dart from wall to wall, chirping and chirping. They perch on the tub and whistle to their young. *Come out! Come out!*

Renata gasps as four tiny wrens march out onto
the shelf. They all look sleepy and exactly alike.

Mama and papa dash to the window frame.
They churr at their little ones. *Fly!*

The fledglings open their wings and
fling themselves into the air. Renata
holds her breath.

Oh, no! One lands on the edge of
the tub and slides in.

A second tilts sharply and drops into the tub.

The others teeter like seesaws
until they too topple in.

Mama and papa scold their brood, but the young wrens do not fly up. Renata crawls over to peer into the tub. The babies are beating their wings, trying to lift off. They are trapped!

"Don't worry," Renata reassures them. "I'll help you."

But how? The tub is too heavy to turn over. And she can't give the wrens flying lessons. Maybe if she could pick them up—but that might frighten them. What if she could build something . . . ?

"I know!" Renata grabs a board. Gently she leans it into the tub.

"Jump on," she whispers. "You can do it."

The baby birds hop onto the plank. Up, up they skitter.

At the tiptop they try their wings again.

This time they glide to the windowsill.

Renata cheers them on silently. Mama and papa wren streak
out over the yard, calling their family to follow. The young
wrens lift their wings like tiny fans and sail out into the world.

Renata runs to the window.

"Goodbye! Goodbye!" she cries as the wrens flit over the
woodpile and disappear into the woods.

Renata turns. She glances around the unfinished
room. It feels so quiet and empty now.

But there is Papi in the doorway. He holds out his
arms and Renata goes into them. "My helper,"
he murmurs. "Come on. Let's get to work."